Recycling Fun!

Mr Bull, the binman, is collecting the rubbish. It's early in the morning so he tries to be as quiet as he can.

Crash Clank!

But Mr Bull is not very good at being quiet.
"Hello Mr Bull," snort Daddy Pig, Peppa and George.

Peppa and George are helping
to clear up the breakfast things.
"We don't put bottles in the rubbish bin.
They can be recycled," says Mummy Pig.

Soon they have collected enough things, so Peppa and her family set off for the recycle centre.

Soon, they arrive at Miss Rabbit's recycle centre.

Miss Rabbit is sitting high up inside a big crane.

She is busy recycling all the rusty old cars.

It is very noisy.

"Who knows which bin the bottles go in?"
asks Mummy Pig.

"And the cans go in the blue one!" says Peppa.

"Well done, Peppa," smiles Mummy Pig.
Rattle! Rattle!

"Where's our car gone?" asks Daddy Pig. "Stand back!" shouts Miss Rabbit from up above them. Miss Rabbit is about to recycle Peppa's car!

"Stop!"
shouts Peppa.
"Our car isn't old
and rusty!"

"Ha Ha! Silly me!" says Miss Rabbit.

"I just love recycling."

"So do we!" laughs Peppa.

"But we also love our little car!"